Words in
Our Hands

Story by Ada B. Litchfield
Pictures by Helen Cogancherry

Albert Whitman & Company, Morton Grove, Illinois

The author and editor wish to thank Ann Hopkins, Framingham, Massachusetts; Debbie Koshelnik Turner, Arlington, Washington; Grace and David Mudgett, Jacksonville, Illinois; Dr. Patricia Scherer of the Glenview Center on Deafness, Glenview, Illinois; Dr. Rachel Mayberry of the Program in Audiology and Hearing Impairment Department, Northwestern University, Evanston, Illinois; and Max Scism of the National Theatre of the Deaf, Eugene O' Neill Theater Center, Waterford, Connecticut.

Library of Congress Cataloging-in-Publication Data

Litchfield, Ada Bassett.
   Words in our hands.

   (A Concept book)
   SUMMARY: Nine-year-old Michael explains the facts and feelings of family life with deaf parents.
   [1. Deaf—Fiction. 2. Physically handicapped—Fiction. 3. Parent and child—Fiction.] I. Cogancherry, Helen. II. Title.
PZ7.L697Wo   [Fic]   79-28402
ISBN 0-8075-9212-9

For Althea and Jim Ross
in memory of Polly,
a self-taught hearing-ear dog.

My name is Michael Turner. I am nine years old. I have two sisters, Gina and Diane, a dog named Polly, and two parents who can't hear me when I talk.

They never have heard me. You see, my mom and dad were born deaf.

Nobody knows for sure why, but it might be because Grandma Ellis had measles before my mother was born and Grandma Turner was in a car accident before my father was born. Sometimes when a mother who is expecting a baby has some disease or is in an accident, the baby is born blind or deaf or is hurt some other way.

My parents never heard any sounds at all when they were babies. Some people think a person who can't hear can't learn to talk. That's not true.

My mom and dad went to a school for deaf kids when they were growing up. That's where they learned to talk. They learned by placing their fingers on their teacher's throat and feeling how words *felt* in her voice box as she said them. They learned how words *looked* by watching her face, especially her lips, as she spoke. It's hard to learn to say words that way. But my parents did.

WHEN MICHAEL'S MOTHER WAS A LITTLE GIRL

They don't talk much now, but they can talk. My mother's voice is high and squeaky. My father's is harsh and loud. My parents have never heard other people talking or even their own voices, so they don't know how voices sound. It's not always easy to understand what they are saying, but Gina and Diane and I can.

Sometimes my mother and father can understand what people are saying by reading their lips. That's another thing my parents learned at their school—lip reading.

Reading lips is hard. Some people don't move their lips much when they talk. Or they hide their mouths with their hands or with a moustache. Besides, many words look alike when you say them. Look in the mirror and say *pin* and *bin*, *hand* and *and*, *hill* and *ill*. See what I mean?

How we move our bodies and what our faces look like when we talk help our parents read our lips. But most of the time we talk to them with our hands as well as our mouths. Grandma Ellis says we have words in our hands.

One way to talk with your hands is to learn a special alphabet so you can spell words with your fingers. This is called *finger spelling*.

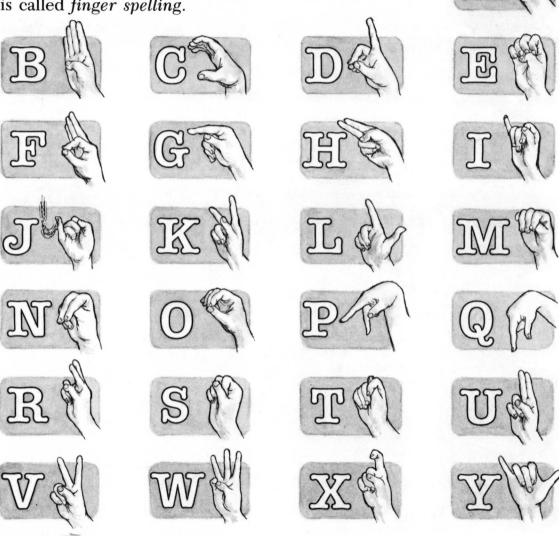

Can you finger spell your name?

Another way to handtalk is to use sign language. Once you have learned sign language, it is easier and faster than finger spelling.

Oh, sure, everybody uses some sign language. You tell your friends to "go away" without using your voice at all. But sign language for the deaf is like French or Spanish. You have to learn many signs that other people understand before you can talk to anybody.

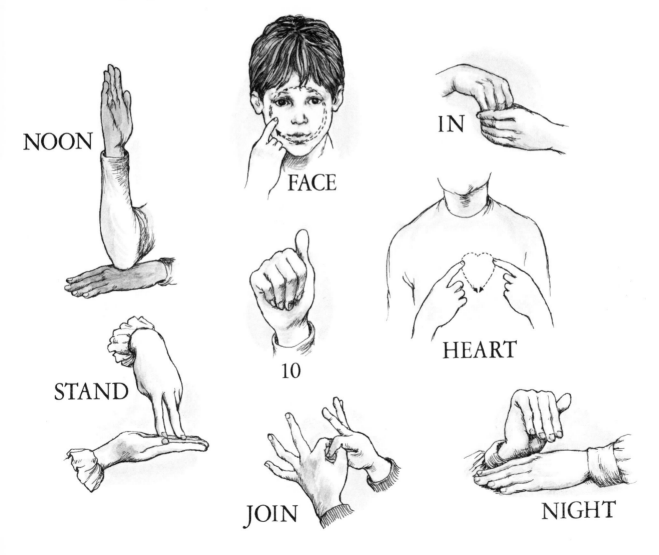

NOON

FACE

IN

STAND

10

HEART

JOIN

NIGHT

Gina, Diane, and I are learning new signs all the time. My mother and father learned sign language when they were little. And they taught us signs when we were babies, just as hearing parents teach their children words. Our grandparents, friends, and neighbors helped us learn to talk.

There are five ways Diane can ask my mother for a peanut butter sandwich.

She can make her mouth move slowly so my mother can read her lips.

She can finger spell *peanut butter* like this:

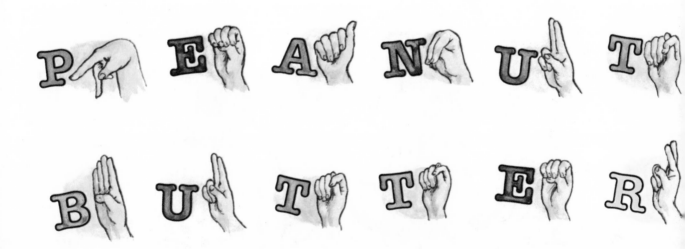

She can ask in sign language. That's easier than finger spelling.

She can print *peanut butter sandwich* on the writing pad my mother always carries with her.

Or she can lead my mother to the jar of peanut butter and point.

My parents have some neat things to help them. In our house, when the telephone or doorbell rings, lights flash on and off. We have a TTY attached to our phone. A TTY is a teletypewriter that spells out messages on tape. Then my parents can type messages back.

Of course, the person calling us has to have a teletypewriter, and not very many people do. That means that many times we kids have to talk on the phone for our parents. And sometimes we have to talk to people who come to the door.

When we were babies, my mother or father checked on us very often to be sure we were all right. They took turns at night. They used a cry alarm, too. A cry alarm is a microphone that is hooked up to a light. When we cried, a light would flash in our parents' bedroom or in the kitchen or living room.

When Diane was little, Gina and I helped take care
of her. We would hear when she cried and tell my
mom or dad.

Some deaf people have a hearing-ear dog to help them. We have Polly. Polly hasn't had lessons in hand signals the way real hearing-ear dogs have. But she can do many things a hearing-ear dog does.

She gets my mother up by tugging at her blankets if her flashing-light alarm doesn't wake her.

She runs back and forth to let my mom and dad
know someone is at the door. She makes a big fuss if a
flashing-light alarm goes off or if a pan is boiling over
on the stove.

When Diane was a baby, Polly helped take care of
her. She still follows Diane around and runs to tell my
mother if Diane gets into trouble.

Just because my parents are deaf doesn't mean we don't do things other families do. We go to church. My mom and dad go to programs at school. We go on picnics. We have friends over for dinner and to stay all night. We drive to the city to the Science Museum.

It isn't true that deaf people can't drive a car. Both my parents drive. They just have to depend on their eyes to avoid accidents. That's why my dad put rear-view mirrors on both sides of our car.

We are a happy family. At least we were until about six months ago. Then the publishing company where my father has always worked moved to a new town, one hundred miles away.

My father is the editor of a magazine about farming. Nobody in the family wanted to move. But my father loves his job so, of course, he wanted to go with his company.

We bought a new house with a big yard that everybody liked, but it took a long time to get used to our new town. Before, my mom had always done all the shopping and banking for our family. Now she felt a little strange going into a store or bank where the clerks didn't know her. Very often she wanted Gina or me to go with her.

In our old town, everybody knew our family. No-body stared when they saw us talking with our hands. But in the new town, people did stare. Of course, they pretended they didn't see us. That was dumb. I knew they were looking.

It was even worse when my mom and dad talked. It seemed as if everyone looked at us when they heard my parents' strange-sounding voices. Sometimes Gina and I felt embarrassed, especially when we had to tell someone what my mother or father had said.

Gina and I didn't want to feel that way. We knew how shy my parents felt. We knew mom missed her art classes. We knew they both missed their old friends. We knew they were as lonesome and homesick as we were!

One awful day I saw three kids making fun of my parents. They were standing behind Mom and Dad and pretending to talk with their hands. I was so upset I wanted to pretend something, too. Just for a minute, I wanted to pretend my mother and father were not my parents. I had never felt that way before.

I was really so ashamed of myself.

That very same day Gina's favorite teacher gave her a note to take home. It was an invitation for our family to go to a performance of the National Theatre of the Deaf.

At first, I didn't want to give the invitation to my parents. I didn't want them to go. I didn't want people to make fun of them or feel sorry for Gina and me.

But Gina said they should go. She said that the play would be in sign language, and who would understand it better than our parents? I knew she was right. Besides, Mom and Dad needed to go out and meet new people.

Still, I was worried about what might happen. The night of the play, all sorts of questions were popping into my mind as I dragged up the steps into the hall. Then I saw those three dumb kids standing in the doorway. One of them grinned and wiggled his fingers at me.

That made me angry! I wanted to give him a good punch in the nose, but I kept going.

The big hall was filled with people. Just inside the
door, my mother signed to me, "Where will we sit?"

To our surprise, a man stood up and said, "There are
five seats over here."

We couldn't believe it. He was talking in sign language!

All around us, people were laughing and talking.
Many of them were talking with their hands. They
didn't seem to care who was watching.

Before the play started, we learned from our program that some of the actors were deaf and some could hear. The hearing actors and some of the deaf actors would speak in the play. All of the actors would sign, sometimes for themselves and sometimes for each other. And sometimes they would all sign together. Everyone in the audience would be able to understand what was going on.

THE NATIONAL THEATRE OF THE DEAF

Presents

The Wooden Boy

The play we saw was called *The Wooden Boy*. It was
about Pinocchio, a puppet who wanted to be a real
boy. It was both funny and sad.

After the play, we went backstage to meet the actors. The deaf performers talked with people who
knew sign language. The hearing actors helped the
other people understand what was being said.

I was proud of my parents. They were smiling, and their fingers were flying as fast as anyone's. For the first time in many months, they seemed to feel at home.

Then we had another surprise. Gina's teacher came over to us. She talked very slowly and carefully so my mother could read her lips. Then she signed with her hands!

Gina was excited. Her favorite teacher, who wasn't deaf, had words in her hands, too. Gina was learning something she didn't know before. We all were. We were learning there were many friendly people in our new town who could talk with our parents. I decided this place wasn't going to be so bad, after all.

I think some of the hearing people around us were learning something too—even those awful kids, who were still following us around.

Maybe they never thought about it before, but being deaf doesn't mean you can't hear or talk. If you have to, you can hear with your eyes and talk with your hands.

I'm glad that Gina and Diane and I know so many signs already. Why don't you learn a few yourself?